Ladybird books are widely available, but in case of difficulty may be ordered by post or telephone from:

Ladybird Books – Cash Sales Department Littlegate Road Paignton Devon TQ3 3BE
Telephone 01803 554761

A catalogue record for this book is available from the British Library

Published by Ladybird Books Ltd Loughborough Leicestershire UK
Ladybird Books Inc Auburn Maine 04210 USA

Wishing Moon

by Lesley Harker

Picture
Ladybird

Persephone Brown was tired of being small. "All I see are feet and knees. I wish I had a pair of stilts," she said, "or a tall giraffe to ride on."

When she went shopping,
she only saw the lowest shelves.

And when she went to the woods,
she could only reach the lowest branches.

And when she went to Grandma's house,
she couldn't even reach the doorknocker!

When it was Christmas,
Persephone Brown asked
Father Christmas for a ladder.

And for her birthday she wanted a flying trapeze.

"Mum," said Persephone, "I'm sick of being small."

"You'll soon grow," said her mum. "Eat your beans, Persephone."

Persephone Brown went into the garden. (She had to ask her mother to open the back door.)

"I HATE BEING SMALL!" she yelled, "I WANT TO BE BIG!"

Because that night it was a Wishing Moon, she got her heart's desire.

All of a sudden Persephone Brown
was HUGE! So huge, she couldn't fit in
the house. She had to live in the garden.

When she stood up she banged her
head on the tree-tops. And when she
sat down she squashed all the rhubarb!

But worst of all she couldn't get into her new red wellies.

"OUCH!" said Persephone, "OUCH! OUCH! BOTHER!"

"Mum," shouted Persephone down the chimney, "I'm tired of being tall."

"Never mind," said her mother, "I expect you'll get used to it. Could you just give the upstairs windows a wipe, dear?"

Persephone Brown yelled up at the Moon, "I've changed my mind," she said, "I wish I was small again."

The Moon tut-tutted to itself. "Some people are never satisfied!"

"Well, I'm sorry," explained Persephone, "but I didn't know being big would be so difficult."

"I'm big," said the Moon, huffily, "I don't find it difficult at all."

"But you don't have to shout at your mum down a chimney," said Persephone. "I don't even fit in my house anymore."

"Never mind, you know fresh air is much better for you," said the Moon. "It builds up your muscles and puts colour in your cheeks."

"But what about my Grandma?" said Persephone. "Now she's old she doesn't see so well. I'm too far away up here."

"Can't you buy her a telescope?" muttered the Moon.

"No!" said Persephone Brown.

"Well at least you can reach her doorknocker now," said the Moon.

"Only if I bend right down and get a crick in my neck!" said Persephone.

"I haven't heard one good reason to change you back again yet," said the Moon to Persephone Brown.

"Because I want my mum to give me a big cuddle and tuck me up in my bed like she used to," she said.

The Moon smiled. "Well of course you do," it said, "and that IS the very best reason I ever heard. You get your wish, Persephone Brown…"

And...

WHOOSH down she went like a popped balloon!

KNOCK! KNOCK! went
Persephone on the front door.

"Who's there?" said Mum.

"Someone just the right size!"
said Persephone Brown.

"Goodnight Wishing Moon."

Picture Ladybird

Books for reading aloud with 2 – 6 year olds

The *Picture Ladybird* range is full of exciting stories and rhymes that are
perfect to read aloud and share. There is something for everyone – animal stories,
bedtime stories, rhyming stories – and lots more!

Ten titles for you to collect

WISHING MOON AGE 3+
written & illustrated by Lesley Harker

Persephone Brown wanted to be BIG. All she ever
saw were feet and knees – it really wasn't on. Then
one special night her wish came true. Persephone
Brown just grew and grew and *GREW…*

DON'T WORRY WILLIAM AGE 3+
by Christine Morton
illustrated by Nigel McMullen

It's a sleepy dark night. A creepy dark night.
A night for naughty bears to creep downstairs and
have an adventure. But, going in search of biscuits
to make them brave, Horace and William hear a
bang – a very loud bang – an On-The-Stairs bang!
Whatever can it be?

BENEDICT GOES TO THE BEACH AGE 3+
written & illustrated by Chris Demarest

It's hot in the city – *really* hot. Poor Benedict just
has to cool off. There is only one thing for it, head
for the beach – *any* beach! Deciding is the easy
part – getting there is another matter altogether…

TOOT! LEARNS TO FLY AGE 3+
by Geraldine Taylor & Jill Harker
illustrated by Georgien Overwater

It's time for Toot to learn to fly, to try and zoom
across the sky. First there's take off – watch it –
steady! Whoops! Bump! He's not quite ready!
Follow Toot's route across the sky and see if he
ever *does* learn to fly!

JOE AND THE FARM GOOSE AGE 2+
by Geraldine Taylor & Jill Harker
illustrated by Jakki Wood

A perfect way to introduce young children to
farmyard life. There is lots to see and talk
about – pigs and their piglets, cows and sheep,
hens in the barn – and Joe's special friend – a very
inquisitive goose!

THE STAR THAT FELL AGE 3+
by Karen Hayles
illustrated by Cliff Wright

When a star falls from the night sky, Fox and all
the other animals want its precious warmth and
brightness. When Dog finds the star he gives it
to his friend Maddy. But as Maddy's dad tells her,
all stars belong to the sky, and soon she must
give it back.

TELEPHONE TED AGE 3+
by Joan Stimson
illustrated by Peter Stevenson

When Charlie starts playgroup poor Ted is left
sitting at home like a stuffed toy. It's not much
fun being a teddy on your own with no one to talk
to. But then – *brring, brring* – the telephone rings,
and that's when Ted's adventure begins.

JASPER'S JUNGLE JOURNEY AGE 3+
written & illustrated by Val Biro

What's behind those rugged rocks? A lion wearing
purple socks! Just one of the strange sights Jasper
encounters as he goes in search of his lost teddy
bear. A delightful rhyming story full of jungle
surprises!

SHOO FLY SHOO! AGE 4+
by Brian Moses
illustrated by Trevor Dunton

If a fly flies by and it's bothering you, just swish it
and swash it and tell it to *shoo!* Trace the trail of
the buzzing, zuzzing fly in this gloriously silly
rhyming story.

GOING TO PLAYGROUP AGE 2+
by Geraldine Taylor & Jill Harker
illustrated by Terry McKenna

Sam's day at playgroup is full of exciting activities.
He's a cook, a mechanic, a pirate and a band
leader… he even flies to the moon! Ideal for
children starting playgroup and full of ideas for
having fun at home, too!